CHRISTOPHER BROWN
Accidental Detective

Written by Valerie Bloom

Illustrated by Monique Steele

Collins

1 Trouble in the village

"Look! Every last one gone!" shouted Mrs Henry.

"Who could have done this?" asked Mr Peart.

"If I catch the culprit – !" Mrs Henry didn't say what she would do.

My sister Jenny and I heard them from a long way off. We looked at each other and started running.

There was a group of people talking and waving angrily.

"What's happened?" I asked

"There was a thief in the village last night."
Mrs Henry pointed to the empty field where yesterday
her sugar canes had been waving in the breeze.

Jenny's eyes widened. "They didn't even leave
one cane?"

"Not a dry stalk. But if I catch them!" Mrs Henry said, angrily. "Jail's too good for them!"

Corporal Watson, the village police officer, was standing next to Mr Peart. He looked at Mrs Henry and shook his head. "My dear Mrs Henry, I hope you're not planning to take the law into your own hands. This is a matter for the police. Just leave it to me. I'll get to the bottom of this in good time."

Jenny tugged at my arm. "C'mon. Dad's waiting for the paper."

"Who do you think could be doing this?" I asked her on the way home.

"I can't think of anyone we know who'd do such a thing," said Jenny.

"It was Mr Mundle's bananas on Tuesday, and now Mrs Henry's sugar canes. So at least we know it's not them."

"Watch out, thieves," Jenny mocked. "Christopher Brown, famous detective is on the case."

Neither of us knew then how true that soon would be.

2 The art competition

I was sitting under the June plum tree in the garden, trying to draw a hummingbird that was feeding from the orange blossoms. It wasn't going well.

The bird wouldn't keep still, and it was difficult to keep the drawing pad steady and draw with one hand while eating the mango I had in the other.

Jenny was sitting on the swing reading the children's section of the newspaper.

"Hey, Chris," she said. "Look at this! There's an art competition here you could enter. You just need to send in some drawings of your community."

"Oh, yeah?" I wasn't that interested in competitions. I took another bite of mango and wiped the juice dribbling down my chin. "What's the prize?"

"The top three entrants will have their artwork exhibited at the National Gallery," she read.

"What!" I sat bolt upright, an unchewed piece of mango hanging from my open mouth.

"Each winner also gets … worth of art supplies from Hobby Palace." She named a sum of money, but I wasn't really listening. My artwork in the National Gallery!

"If only – " I said dreamily.

"You know people round here think you're strange because you do nothing but draw pictures all day long. Here's your chance to show them how good you are."

3 The birthday gift

"Here," Mum said, handing me a packet.
"It's a birthday present from your Aunt Madge."

"But my birthday was last week!"

"Yes, but your dad only saw her when he went to the city yesterday. She didn't want to send it in the post."

I shook the packet. "What is it?"

"You won't know until you open it," Jenny said.

I took a bite of roast breadfruit and started unwrapping the present. "Why's Dad not having breakfast with us?"

"There was a visitor on the farm last night. He's gone to the police station to report it."

I stopped chewing. "What did they take?"

"All the mangoes."

"What? All of them? The Milly mangoes too?"

Mum nodded and I groaned. "Man! I love those Milly mangoes! I wish Corporal Watson would hurry up and catch the thief."

"Never mind." Mum nodded towards my present. I unwrapped the packet and gasped. "No way!"

"What is it?" Jenny and Mum spoke together.

I held it with trembling hands. "Look what Aunt Madge sent me!"

"Wow! That's so cool!" Jenny held out her hand. "Can I see?"

Reluctantly, I handed over the phone in its gleaming black case. "Don't drop it!"

"You're so lucky!" Jenny handed me the phone. "I haven't got a phone and I'm older than you." She was looking expectantly at Mum who pretended not to notice.

"We'll have to put some parental controls on it before you can use it," Mum said.

"OK."

"And you know you're not allowed to take it to school, don't you?" Jenny said.

"I know." I had the whole holidays to use it, and nothing could spoil my happiness.

4 Snap happy

For the next few days, I spent every free minute on my phone. I discovered artists I'd never heard about – Augusta Savage, Kara Walker and Jacob Lawrence. I learnt some interesting things about the most famous artists, too.

"Hey, Jenny!" I called to my sister. "Did you know that Picasso was accused of stealing the Mona Lisa?"

"Really?" Jenny's voice sounded bored.

"Yeah! And Dalí thought he was his dead brother!"

"Interesting."

"Did you know Leonardo da Vinci was a pro – pro-crast – in-at … or? What does that mean?"

"Procrastinator. Someone who keeps putting things off. A bit like you, really. Shouldn't you be getting some drawings done for the competition?"

"Oh yes!" I said. "I'll go take some photos of our neighbours."

Jenny looked puzzled. "Why do you need photos? It's a drawing competition."

"Who's going to sit still for hours while I draw them? I'll need photos to draw from, won't I?"

I set off down the road, phone in hand.

"Boy, will you stop pointing that thing in my face!"
Mrs Henry didn't want her picture taken.

"No, thank you. Not today," Mr Peart said.

The boys in my class weren't interested either.
"Forget that, Christopher. Come play football with us.
We need one more person to make up the side."

"Nobody wants their picture taken!" I moaned
to Jenny later. "I might as well forget about
the competition."

"You give up too quickly. Just take some pictures of
the village and if people happen to accidentally get in
the picture, well – "

"Jenny," I said, "you're a genius!"

I walked towards the river at the back of my school.
Mr Johnson, our head teacher, was painting the door
of his office. He wouldn't mind if I took a picture of
his office.

Opposite the school was the house of Mr Blake, the caretaker. Mr Blake was standing on his veranda, eyes closed, head thrown back, left hand flung wide, right hand holding an imaginary microphone. He was singing. "... Down by the riverside!"

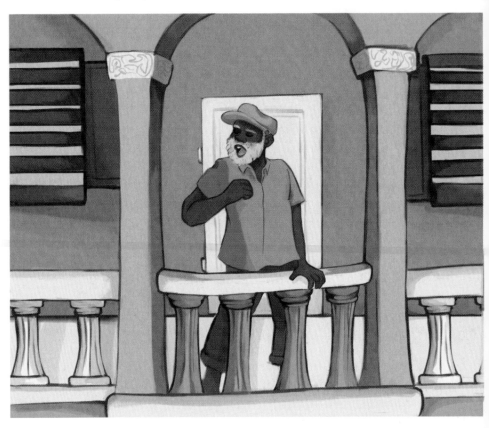

Perfect picture. Soon I had all the photographs I needed. The next morning I hurried to the post office and sent off my entry to the competition.

5 The letter

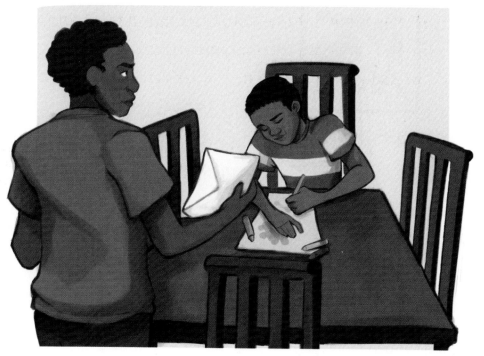

The following week I was drawing in the dining room when Dad came in. "Chris, you've got a letter." Dad dropped the letter onto the table. "Looks important," he said, eyebrows raised.

I picked up the envelope, heart pounding. I never got letters. Could it be … ?

"It would be easier to read if you opened it, you know?" Dad said.

My hands were shaking.

Dear Christopher,

Congratulations!

Your entry in the My Community art competition was judged among the top three and will be published in The Daily Record on Wednesday 13th.

Along with the other two winners, you will be invited to exhibit your work in the National Gallery next March. Your voucher for art supplies from Hobby Palace will be sent to you soon.

We were all very impressed with your artwork and would welcome more work from you for our Children's Corner.

X _____   X _____

I showed the letter to Dad.

"I won!"

I jumped out of my chair and ran out into the yard
where Jenny and Mum were sitting under the orange
tree, peeling ginger.

"Jenny! Mum!" I shouted. "I won."

6 A spot of bother

On Wednesday morning, Dad went to get the paper. My family had proudly told the whole village about my success and everyone had promised to buy the paper. I was a local hero, Jenny said.

We'd gathered around the dining table and Dad was opening the paper when there was a shout at the gate. We trooped onto the veranda. It was Mrs Henry and she didn't look happy.

"Mr Brown, I want a word with your son."
Mrs Henry shoved the folded newspaper under
Dad's nose. "Look at me! My hair uncombed, my
frock wet. I look a mess."

Dad didn't have a chance to say anything.
There was another shout from the gate and Mr Blake
the caretaker came striding into the yard, waving
his newspaper.

"Look!" He held up the paper so we could all see.
There was a choking sound behind me and I looked
round to see Jenny trying in vain to stifle her laughter.

"I didn't have my teeth in! Now the whole world knows I have none!"

The gate rattled again. It was Corporal Watson, the police officer.

"Mr Brown, you need to have a word with young Christopher."

I didn't understand why Corporal Watson was so angry. His picture wasn't that bad. He was only picking his nose.

Dad's face looked like the sky just before one of our tropical storms.

Our yard was getting very crowded. Angry voices were competing to be heard.

"My nose is never that big!"

"I was still in my pyjamas!"

"I was only taking a short nap under the guinep tree. Now I look like I'm lazy!"

I inched towards the living room, slipped through the door and ran.

I sat on a boulder and dangled my bare feet in the water. Although it was only mid-morning, the sun was already blazing down and the cool water calmed my heated feelings, but only slightly.

It was all Jenny's fault. Stupid competition! I wished I'd never heard of it. I kicked the water angrily, drenching myself. That brought me to my senses.

It wasn't Jenny's fault. I really wanted to win that competition. I had won! I'd have my work hanging in the National Gallery! I flung my hands to the sky and whooped with joy.

"Yessss!"

A flock of parakeets in the top of the coconut tree flew away, screeching in annoyance.

I stood up. Time to go home. By now the angry crowd would be gone. I had some drawing to do and artwork to work on if I was going to be ready for my exhibition. I smiled as I thought about that. My own exhibition in the National Gallery!

7 No more drawing

I was still smiling as I mounted the steps onto
the veranda. Mum was on the chaise longue and
Dad was sitting on the rocking chair, the newspaper
in his hand. He looked up as I approached. Our eyes
met and my smile disappeared. I glanced at Mum
and her eyes avoided mine. She got up and went into
the house without a word. My heart sank.

I didn't know it was possible to be so miserable.
Dad told me that Corporal Watson had told him he
was a bad parent – in front of half the village.

He didn't seem angry, but I knew I was in
big trouble. Suddenly, in the middle of telling me all
this, he asked, "Did you pick up the cocoa shells from
the farm?" My hand flew to my mouth. I'd forgotten.

"No? How about giving the goats water in
the morning?"

He saw the answer in the look on my face.
I'd forgotten to do that too. I'd been too busy
collecting ideas for my artwork.

"Did you tie out the goats this morning?"

"Yes, sir." At least I'd remembered to do that!

"You know, Christopher, Mr Matthews came to see
me this morning."

"But I didn't draw him!"

Dad continued as if he hadn't heard. "He was the only one who didn't come to complain about his picture in the paper."

I let out a sigh of relief.

"Instead, he came to complain about my goats which had eaten all his cabbages."

"But I tied – " And then I remembered. I had been about to tie the goats when I'd seen the mongoose. It would be a perfect addition to the pictures of the other animals in my portfolio. By the time I'd got my phone out, it had scooted away up the bank and I'd followed.

Dad nodded. "It seems to me you've been too distracted lately, Christopher, so I'm going to help you out. Go and bring me all your art materials. No more drawing and no more photographs until you learn to be more responsible. And then we'll go to the farm. We have work to do."

8 A thief in the night

Very early the next morning I got out of bed. I was going to take some photographs of the sunrise. I put on my clothes over my pyjamas. It would be chilly this early in the morning.

The village was still fast asleep and I knew there'd be no one about.

I stepped quietly through the house gently easing open the back door. I stopped to make sure no one had heard me. I didn't want to wake anyone.

Outside, the air
smelt of night jasmine,
oleanders and
rose apples.
    The light from the full
moon was so bright it
was like daytime.
    It didn't take me long
to reach the little hill
and I stopped beneath
a star-apple tree.
From there I had a clear
view over the yam
field towards the hills
where the sun rose.
While I was waiting,
I thought I'd take some
pictures of the yam
field and the trees
in the moonlight.
With the moon so bright
I wouldn't even need to
use the flash.

Suddenly, one of the shadows began to move.
A shadow with wings!

My heart raced. My mouth became as dry
as sawdust. I wanted to run but my feet had turned
to jelly. I opened my mouth to shout for help but no
sound came.

I pressed myself into the trunk of the tree and closed
my eyes. Perhaps by the time I opened them again
the thing would be gone.

It was still there when I opened my eyes
a second later. I wished I'd stayed in bed.

The shadow moved towards the yam field and a moonbeam played across its face.

I gasped in shock. I couldn't believe my eyes. Immediately, the shadow stopped. He looked towards where I was trying to melt into the tree. I held my breath, hoping that the navy tee-shirt and black trousers I had on would just look like a part of the tree trunk.

He waited. When there was no sound, he moved towards the yam field and started to dig.

What I'd thought were wings turned out to be two large sacks and into these he was stuffing the yams he'd dug up. My father's yams. This was the village thief! No one would believe me if I told them who it was.

I wanted to run out and stop him, but I was scared. He was big and strong and had tools and all I had was a phone. My phone! I could phone Dad. But not without the thief hearing.

There was nothing to stop me photographing him though. The phone camera was silent. I took photograph after photograph without a sound.

When he'd finished, he hoisted one sack onto his head and lifted the other over his back.

Then my heart stopped. He was coming straight towards me.

I couldn't move. As he drew nearer, my fingers tightened around my phone.

Then, just before he got to the tree, he turned right. He scrambled down the slope and disappeared. A few minutes later, I heard a vehicle driving off. I ran.

I was shaking as I crawled into bed.

I had to let everyone know who the thief was. The whole world should know. If I called a meeting of the village probably no one would come and they would think I'd made it up anyway.

Then I remembered my letter from the newspaper and knew just what I'd do. They'd said they would like to see some more of my artwork. Well, I had some artwork on my phone. I'd name it "A thief in the night".

9 Accidental detective

We were eating breakfast the following Wednesday when there was a shout at the gate.

We went out to the veranda. My head teacher and the caretaker were standing in the yard.

"Mr Brown," said my head teacher, pushing a newspaper into Dad's hands, "I'd like to have a word with your son."

I groaned. Not again.

He turned to me. "Christopher Brown, come here and let me shake your hand."

Puzzled, I glanced at Dad. He was reading with a look of disbelief, a small smile tickling the corner of his mouth.

I began to relax.

"I want you to know that you can take my photo any time," Mr Blake said. "Teeth or no teeth."

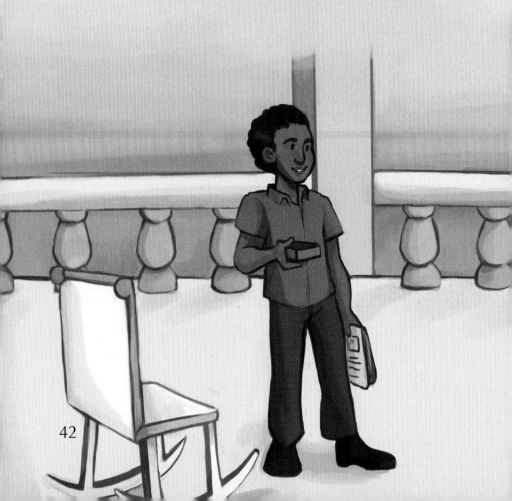

More people were coming up to the house.
Big smiles on their faces.

"Well done, son!" said Dad. "But how – "

They sat me down and I told them the whole story.
How I'd gone to take photographs and caught
Corporal Watson stealing Dad's yams.

Dad went into the house. When he returned, he was
carrying the box I'd given him. He was smiling.

"Here. I think you're going to need this."

"Who would have guessed?" said Jenny.
"The policeman, a thief!"

"Yes," said Mrs Henry. "We were reporting the thief
to the thief!" Everyone laughed.

On Friday morning there was another shout at
the gate. "Mr Brown, we'd like a word with your son."

"This is becoming a habit," Mum muttered as we
trooped onto the veranda.

"What – " Dad stopped. The whole village was in
our yard.

My head teacher stepped forward. "Christopher Brown, as a token of our appreciation, we would like to present you with this gift."

It was a large watercolour art set and an easel.

"We can't have our hero preparing for an important exhibition without the best equipment."

"Of course!" said Dad. "You've got a lot of preparation to do, haven't you? You'd best take a holiday from your chores until after the exhibition."

It was the best day of my life!

How did Christopher become a detective?

 Ideas for reading

Written by Gill Matthews
Primary Literacy Consultant

Reading objectives:
- check that the text makes sense to them, discussing their understanding and explaining the meaning of words in context
- ask questions to improve their understanding of a text
- draw inferences such as inferring characters' feelings, thoughts and motives from their actions, and justify inferences with evidence
- predict what might happen from details stated and implied

Spoken language objectives:
- ask relevant questions to extend their understanding and knowledge
- use relevant strategies to build their vocabulary
- articulate and justify answers, arguments and opinions
- participate in discussions, presentations, performances, role play, improvisations and debates

Curriculum links: Relationships education – Respectful relationships

Interest words: raced, pressed, played, hoisted

Build a context for reading

- Ask children to look closely at the front cover and to read the title. Ask what the title means to them.
- Read the back-cover blurb. Explore their understanding of it. Ask what they think the village crimes might be. Ask why they think Christopher Brown might need to do photo research in order to enter an art competition.
- Draw attention to the story being contemporary. Discuss any previous experiences of reading contemporary stories and what their features are.

Understand and apply reading strategies

- Read pp2–5 aloud, using appropriate expression. Discuss where the children think the story is set.
- Ask children to read pp6–12. Discuss what they have noticed that tells them this is a contemporary story. What did they think about the present that Christopher has received?